For Dylan Beech

First published 2008 by Macmillan Children's Books
This edition published in 2012 by Macmillan Children's Books
a division of Macmillan Publishers Limited
20 New Wharf Road, London N1 9RR
Basingstoke and Oxford
Associated companies throughout the world
www.panmacmillan.com

ISBN: 978-1-4472-1003-0 (pb)

Text and illustrations copyright © Tor Freeman 2008

The right of Tor Freeman to be identified as the author and illustrator
of this work has been asserted by her in accordance
with the Copyright, Designs and Patents Act 1988.

1 3 5 7 9 8 6 4 2

A CIP catalogue record for this book is available from the British Library.

Printed in China

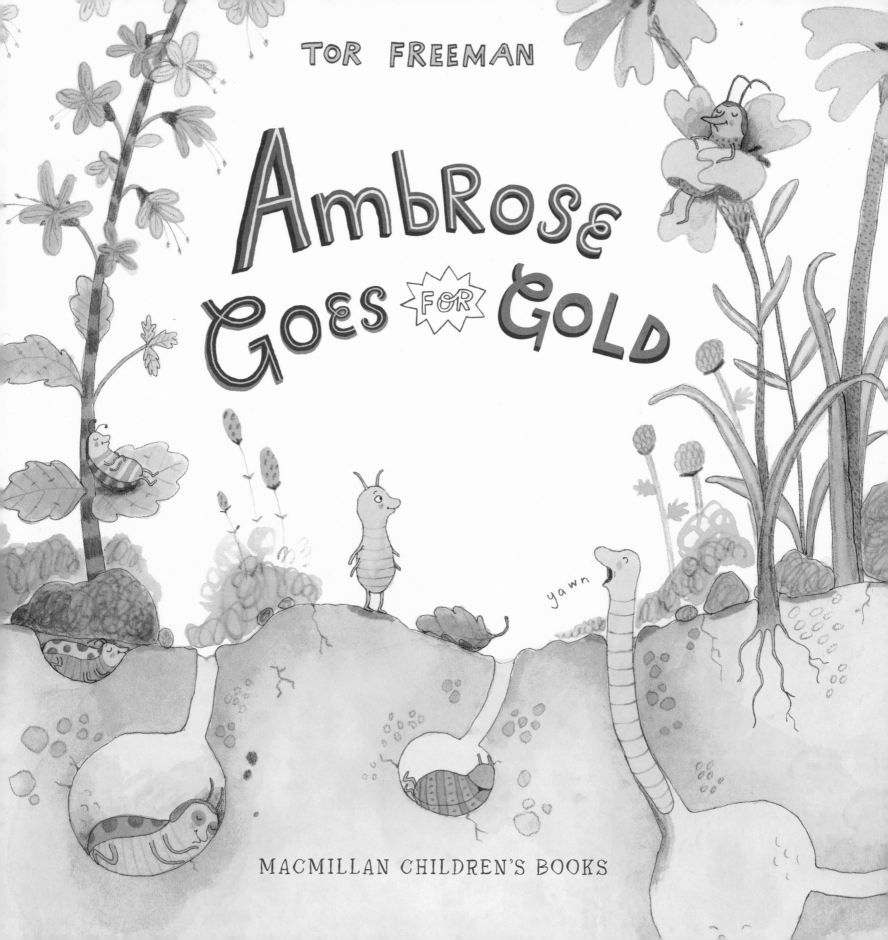

It was a beautiful sunny morning and
Ambrose had been awake since dawn.
He was far too excited to sleep.

GREAT INSECT GAMES

a bit higher

It was the day of the Great Insect Games,
and for the very first time Ambrose
was big enough to compete.

He couldn't wait to win a shiny gold medal,
and had been practising very hard.

Ambrose had done his

lifting

and stretching,

toning

and firming.

He had even done his
to-ing and his fro-ing.

"I wonder which game I will win?"
said Ambrose.

"I am sure to be the best at
something."

As Ambrose arrived, the judge called the insects to gather round. "Welcome to the Great Insect Games!" he cried. "Today's first event will be the Long Jump."

"Hooray!" said Ambrose.
"I'm a good jumper."
And he did some little hops for practice.

Ambrose watched the leaf beetle skitter.

He watched the ant leap.

And when it was Ambrose's turn...

he jumped very far!

But nobody could jump further
than the grasshopper.

Wow!

"Oh no," sighed Ambrose.
He felt very disappointed.

"Don't feel sad," said the kindly grasshopper.
"I am a grasshopper and jumping is what I do
best. Everybody is good at something."

weee!

Don't want
to

"Well," thought Ambrose,
"I may not be a good jumper,
but I expect I'm a good skater."

And, feeling much brighter,
he strode over to the pond.

The Water Skating Contest had just begun, and Ambrose watched the insects glide round and round.

"Well, this looks easy," he thought.

But, oh dear!

It wasn't easy.

OOF!

"Don't worry," said the pond skater,
helping Ambrose out of the water.
"I am a pond skater and skating is
what I do best."

"Well," thought Ambrose,
"I may not be a good skater,
but I know I'm a good runner."

And off he went to join the race.

BANG! They were off...

The butterfly was fast,

GO CENTY!

GOOD LUCK!

but the ladybird
was faster,

and Ambrose was faster still!
He raced towards the finish …

But nobody was as fast
as the tiger beetle.

"Oh dear!" puffed Ambrose.
He had been so close.
"Chin up," said the tiger beetle.
"We tiger beetles are always fast.
Running is what we do best."

"Well," thought Ambrose, "I may not be fast
enough but I'm sure to be strong enough."
He felt ready to win the Strongbug Contest.

The grain of sand?
No problem!

The berry?
A bit more puff.

Next came the acorn . . .

Ambrose strained,

and he pushed,

NRRGH!

and he pulled his very hardest.

But that acorn would not budge.

"Good try, Ambrose," said the rhino beetle. "But a rhino beetle is a strong beetle, and pushing and lifting is what we do best."

"Don't worry," he said.
"Your turn will come."

But time was running out and
Ambrose was getting tired.

"One last chance," he whispered
as he braced himself for the
Loud Noise Competition.

Oh, what a lot of noise!

The worm warbled...

LA LA
LA

BUZZZZZ

the bee buzzed...

CLICK
CLAP
CLAP

and Ambrose made
such a clatter.

But nobody was as
noisy as the cicada.

EEEEEEEEEEE

"I suppose being noisy is what
cicadas do best," said Ambrose
in his smallest, saddest voice.

Ambrose walked slowly away.

"Everyone has a gold medal,"
he sniffed. "Everyone except me.
I'm just not good at anything."

"My legs are not springy,
and I fall over when I skate.
I can't run quickly
and I'm not that strong.
I'm not even very noisy!"

Feeling tired and unhappy,
Ambrose sat down and
nibbled on a twig.

It was a nice twig,
so he had another.

And another.

And then another.

Suddenly there came a loud voice.

"And the winner of the
Twig Eating Competition is . . .

...AMBROSE!"

It was the judge! Ambrose had won!
He had really won his very own,
very shiny gold medal.

"HIP, HIP, HOORAY FOR AMBROSE!"
all the insects cried.

"We knew you could do it,"
said the kindly grasshopper.
"But how did you know?" asked Ambrose.

Everyone laughed.
"Because, Ambrose, you're a
TERMITE. And EATING
is what termites do best!"

As the sun went down, the fireflies came out and the celebrations began. Ambrose danced until his little legs tingled.

"That grasshopper was right," thought Ambrose. "Everybody really is good at something!"

"But I might practise my
skating for next year
... just in case."